Siouxie

Thank you for being a tippity top friend

Love ya heaps

Emma xxx

Like Joy In Season, Like Sorrow

Like Joy In Season, Like Sorrow

MARY DORCEY

salmonpoetry

Published in 2001 by
Salmon Publishing Ltd,
Cliffs of Moher, Co. Clare, Ireland
http://www.salmonpoetry.com
email: info@salmonpoetry.com

Copyright © Mary Dorcey, 2001

ISBN 1 903392 17 9   Paperback

The Arts Council
An Chomhairle Ealaíon

Salmon Publishing gratefully acknowledges the financial
assistance of The Arts Council / An Chomhairle Ealaíon

All rights reserved. No part of this publication may be reproduced or transmitted in any
form or by any means, electronic or mechanical, including photography, recording, or
any information storage or retrieval system, without permission in writing from the
publisher. The book is sold subject to the condition that it shall not, by way of trade or
otherwise, be lent, resold or otherwise circulated without the publisher's prior consent in
any form of binding or cover other than that in which it is published and without a similar
condition, including this condition, being imposed on the subsequent purchaser.

Cover photography by Ilsa Thielan
Cover design and typesetting by Siobhán Hutson
Printed by Offset Paperback Mfrs., PA

In Memorium
Kate Cruise O'Brien

Acknowledgements

With profound gratitude to Dr. Mary Pender for care beyond the call of duty. To my agent Ros Edwards and, as always, with love to Monica.

Contents

1 *Uncharted Passage*

Uncharted Passage	3
Each Day Our First Night	5
Grist to the Mill	8
Going Home Without You	10
The Poet and Satire	12
Knowing What's Best.	14
Sentinel	16
Family Secrets	18
Fairy Tales	19
Landscape	21
Sea Bed	22
On The Tree Top	23
The Streets of Town	25
Sweet Melancholy	28
Making Small Talk	31
Frost	35
Snow	36
Testing the Waters	38

2 *The Rapture of Senses*

These Days of Langour	45
Nocturne	46
Summer	48
The Rapture of Senses	49
Waking	51
Angels at Play	52
Strong Tea	55
Heaven's Breath Held	56
Keeping Vigil	64
Grace	66

3   *Time Has Made a Mirror*

Time Has Made a Mirror	71
Shoulder	72
Once	73
In Your Shoes	75
Blood	76
Learning by Heart	77
Endless Days	79

ONE

Uncharted Passage

Uncharted Passage

You are the flagship –
gladly or not
we travel in your wake.

So long as the masthead
bears your colours
we hold course.

Though you founder,
almost, in this
uncharted passage

Where storm and shallows
threaten alike. Though
we stand-to helpless

While half a lifetime's
cargo is jettisoned
and the flotsam

Of memory; the silks
and the bric-a-brac,
float out,

On an ebb tide. Yet,
so long as you endure
we are young.

So long as you hoard
a remnant of self
above water,

A frail bulwark
survives.
In late middle-age

We remain, all
of us – somebody's
children, still.

Each Day Our First Night

What a beautiful mother
I had –
Forty years ago,
When I was young
And in need of a mother.
Tall and graceful,

Dark haired,
Laughing.
What a fine mother, I had
When I was young.
Now I climb the steps
To a cold house

And call out a word
That used to summon her.
An old woman
Comes to the door:
Gaunt eyed, grey haired,
Feeble. An old woman

Who might be
Anybody's mother. She
Fumbles with the locks,
And smiles a greeting
As if the name spoken
Belonged to her.

We go inside
And I make tea.
The routine questions
Used to prompt her
Fall idle.
She cannot remember

The day of the week,
The hour, nor
The time of year.
Look at the grass,
I say,
Look at the leaves –

You tell me!
Autumn, she answers
At last. Her hands
Wind in her lap,
Her eyes like a child's,
Full of shame.

Each day,
A little more
Is lost of her.
Captured for an instant,
Then gone.
Everything that

Made her particular,
Withering, like leaf
From the tree.
Her love of stories
And song, her wit,
The flesh on her bones.

What a beautiful mother
I had, forty years ago
When I was young
And in need of a mother.
Proud, dark haired
Laughing.

Now I descend the path
From a cold house,
An old woman
Follows to the window,
An old woman
Who might be

Anybody's mother.
She stands patiently
To wave me off –
Remembering
The stage directions,
Of lifted hand

And longing gaze.
In this
Experimental piece –
Each day,
Our first night –
She plays her part

With such command –
Watching her
Take a last bow
From the curtain –
You could swear she
Was born for it!

Grist to the Mill

All grist to the mill,
You say, or at least,
That's how I console
Myself, for wasting so
Much of your precious
Time. I have to remind
My brain, consciously –
That a writer can make
Use of everything.

I sit on the edge
Of the hospital bed,
Lifting the spoon
To your mouth.
Nothing is wasted,
You say,
No experience,
However dismal –
Entirely redundant.
I wipe your chin
With the napkin
Isn't that true?
You ask me,
Wanting it to be.

And thus you offer –
And I resolve
To make it so –
To take this sorrow –
This irreparable loss;
The erasure
By stealth,
Of culture and past –
This commonplace and
Unreported suffering,
And put them to work.

To take your laughter,
Your bafflement, the
Sudden shafts of vision,
Your dark ironies –
And shape them –
Honing them
Into an artefact –
Something
One can take up
And put down.
Something that
Can be looked at
And looked away from.

Unlike this –
This sly dispossession –
This infant dependence
And fear, which
Even your gallows humour,
And that
Family heirloom –
Pride,
Will not mask.
And which once seen
I cannot unsee.

And so I determine
To use them – the
Damage and indignities,
Piled day by day, onto
The wreckage of self.
To put them to service –
Like a scrap and bone
Monger –
Grist to the mill.
For your sake –
For mine.

Going Home Without You

Sometimes it seems
You are playing a game –
An over long joke,
Your white hair
Your cane,
Your shambling step.
Forgetting your birthday.
Your mother's death.

I want to shake you
And say – enough is enough.
Stop this charade
This carnival trick!
At the end of my tether,
Just as you were,
Remember –
When we were children

Playing disguises
And none of us knew
When to stop.
The worst of it all
Is to know that you
Are in there, still –
Exactly as always –
Under this mask

You have adopted –
This pantomime face
Of decay and confusion.
You are in there –
Perfectly you.
Serene and farseeing,
Enjoying the jest.
Like a contrary playmate

When we were young –
Playing 'Hide and Go Seek',
Or 'Blind Man's Bluff'
The one who, defiant,
Refused to give in, who
Clung to concealment
Long past bed time
Or humour. And,

However well, I
Recognise – now as then,
That it is useless
To argue or cajole,
Still the invocations
Rise unsought
From a lost treasury
Of barter and bribe:

Come on now – it's late
We all want our tea.
What will the others think?
Give up now or else!
It's nearly dark
We have to go.
If you can't be good
We won't play again.

Obstinate, contradictory
Child – you'd try
The patience of a saint!
If you don't come out
This instant!
I'm warning you –
I'll leave you here
And go home without you.

The Poet and Satire

'What is this life so full of care
We have no time to stand and stare.
No time to stand beneath the boughs
And stare as long as sheep or cows.'

You are eating lunch at the kitchen
Table. I am washing the dishes.
You are gazing into the garden,
There's something familiar

About that garden, you say,
Holding your fork in the air
Forgetting to eat. There certainly
Ought to be – you've been looking

At it for sixty years, I reply.
I am washing dishes at the kitchen
Sink. You are holding your fork
In the air, neglecting to eat.

Have I? you ask, sceptical,
But not enough to argue the point.
Isn't it an amazing thing –
Memory, the tricks it plays.

Why should I remember that
Poem after all these years
And forget so much else?
I am washing dishes at the

Kitchen sink. You are playing
With lunch at the kitchen table,
Too thoughtful to eat. It would be
A wonderfully interesting study,

My condition, you say, if I
Could stand back and observe it.
Finish your dinner before it's
Cold, I answer. I am washing

Dishes at the kitchen sink.
I always thought it was
A satiric poem, you say. Would
You call it a satiric poem?

The poet must be laughing
At himself, surely, to write
'And stare as long as sheep
Or cows?' I am washing dishes

At the kitchen sink. Who cares
What kind of poem it is, I think.
I have the housework to do.
Look at the beautiful white

Rose by the fence, you say,
The last rose of summer!
I am washing dishes at the
Kitchen sink. I do not care

About satire or roses. Have
You finished your broccoli?
I ask. You are gazing into
The autumn garden (something

Familiar about it, you know)
Who would guess, you
Remark, after a moment's pause,
That you were the well known poet –

I say – look at the beautiful
Rose – the last of summer.
And what do you say? Have you
Finished your broccoli!

Knowing What's Best.

I wish I was going to lunch
With you instead, you say
When I drop you at the
Restaurant door. You gaze
Ahead through the windscreen,
Not into my eyes,

So that I can pretend
Not to notice the longing.
You're a small child again,
Uncertain,
As the first day at school.
Frightened to set out alone,

To make the vast journey
Across a street to a roomful
Of strangers; away from me.
Your friend is waiting.
I say – go now. I pull
On your gloves carefully,

Shifting them over the
Swollen bones of the wrist.
Don't open your bag
Until you get inside.
Mind your money
And your scarf.

You hesitate, as if
I might still, relent
And let you stay home.
I almost say
You're a big girl now
Stand on your own feet.

You hear without my speaking
And set out unsteady but
Brave. A determined child,
Clutching handbag and stick.
You cross the footpath
Intent, counting each step.

Your white head turned
From the daughter of forty
Who waits in the car
Implacable,
Knowing what's best.
Her heart in her mouth.

Sentinel

All through the day –
the labyrinth of hours,
two sets of eyes
keep track of you.

Their green
and brilliant gaze
fixed sentinel
on your wanderings,

From early till late.
Reminding you
of your presence
by theirs.

In the morning when
you come down first
'Very through other',
as they say in Donegal.

Which may or may not
be true. Who knows?
Certainly not you –
very through other,

On these winter mornings
of your eighty-seventh
year, there they sit –
your two companions

Poised in their brindled
shawls, (so alike you
call them – our cat)
gazing from their perch

On the white fridge top.
Half the time,
I don't know
who she is, you say.

But she always
knows me. That's the
astonishing thing
about cats!

Family Secrets

She sits aground
In her kitchen –
A strange world to her now –
Topsy turvy.
Safer to sit.
Where do I keep the teapot?
Who owns that cat,
Do you think?
What day is it?
What are we doing here?
Are we waiting for Christmas
Or past it?
How many children did I have?
Five!
Are you certain?
And did I have them all
With your father?
Isn't that strange –
I had the feeling
There was someone else
As well –
And was wondering
That I
Could have been
So dissolute!

Fairy Tales

Washing your feet,
These days, I remember
When you used to bath us –
Once upon a time –

The three youngest
Together – a plastic boat
Buzzing on the water –
Scrubbing our backs

While we showered each
Other, our thumbs held
Under the running tap.
You swore when you combed

The tangles from our hair.
You sang while you dried us.
Now, I lift your swollen feet
From the basin and wrap them

With a towel, in silence.
Always dry between the
Toes, you used to say. But
I cannot. They are moulded

Together, inseparable. You
Have become web footed, like
The princess in the story
– a once beautiful child,

Cursed by the Fates because
She grew enchanted with her
Own image in the looking-glass
And could not turn her eyes

From its reflection. For
Punishment she was changed
Into a black swan and set to
Wander an ice-filled world,

Forever banished from her own
Form. One of those daughters
Of misfortune, one of many –
Turned to water or to stone,

That once upon a time, we
Girls were warned about in
The fairy tales, our father
Read to us at bedtime.

Landscape

Her eyes stare
Into the distance.
Her hands restless
In her lap.
Memories sprout
From the fissures
In her face,
Like grass
In a graveyard.

Sea Bed

You took me to the beach.
We stood on the shore.
Sand groaned,
The wind railed.

When I put my hand
Into the pocket
Of your coat,
A vast world
Opened –
Dark,
Enclosing.

My fist sank
To the bottom
Like stone
Through water,
And came to rest
On the rough cloth
Of the sea bed.

On The Tree Top

Whenever I was tired
I climbed into your lap
and rested there.

Whenever I was tired
or just because
I wanted to.

I remember how large
and roomy it seemed, the
pool made by your skirt.

Whenever you sat down
I climbed onto your knee
to make use of you –

After dinner, in the
park, at the pictures,
during Mass.

Whenever I was tired
or just because
I wanted to,

I climbed into your lap.
as if you were a tree top
or a carriage.

Your hands were large
and comforting –
I pulled them about me

Like a quilt, and
with one ear turned
to the rhythmic chant

Of adult talk
not yet understood.
The other tuned inwards

To catch
the secret language
of the heart.

I fell asleep, there,
in the valley
made by your skirts.

The Streets of Town

Walking the streets
of the town, in winter
or in summer

From shop to shop –
with you –
getting the messages.

We would stop to talk
to neighbours and friends –
all of them women –

Other housewives
making the most
of an hour's freedom.

The centre point
of their day. Some of
them kept you for

Ten minutes, nattering.
I would tug at your hand,
jerking it like a bell-pull

Whispering up the sleeve
of your coat:
Can we go home, now!

Some you wanted
to escape as much as I
did, the long-winded,

The complaining.
Others swooped down
like birds from the sky,

Fluttered about us,
for an instant,
chirruping and were gone.

One or two
kept you until the clock
struck noon. Turning

To leave, at last,
you would murmur –
Isn't she a lovely woman!

Your tone wistful,
full of delight.
I would gaze after her –

Wanting to understand
what you meant.
Trying to recapture

What had passed –
the magic of surface
and sound: subtlety

In a turn of phrase,
the sensuous movement
of a hand. Is that

When I first learned
to notice (waiting
for you to be finished

Talking to your friends)
is that where I learned
to value above all —

The indefinable moments
of grace that kept you
standing in the street,

On a summer's day
ignoring me —
sudden laughter

In a woman's voice
or eyes that caught
the light in such a way —

A sudden trick of shadow
seemed to unveil
a window to the heart.

Sweet Melancholy

Elegies,were what you sang
While you washed the delph,
Narratives of lost love
Or of a nation betrayed,
Gazing out the scullery
Window to the garden,to the
Sycamore and the rockery.
(I loved those words –
Delph and rockery.)
'The summer's gone and

All the roses falling.'
At five,(the last of five)
I sat beside you with
Colouring book and crayons
And learned for the first
Time, the persuasions of
Metaphor. 'Alas and well may
Erin weep that Connaught
Lies in slumber deep,'
Words and melody enthralled

Me – the soft laments,the
Enigmatic stories. One
Song, in particular lured
My imagination and roused
A luscious melancholy.
The air was ominous, yet
Sweet and there was a shadow
Cast by it, over the verses
That I could not fathom.
'I know where I'm going and

I know who's going with me...'
The tension that fell
Between sense and sound
Baffled and delighted me:
'I know who I love but the
Dear knows who I'll marry...'
Where was she going, I wanted
To know, and who did she love?
And hearing repeated, the
Even, liturgical rhythm,

The picture that rose to
My eyes (for what reason?)
Was one I remember still:
I saw a funeral procession;
A coffin borne through the
Streets. I heard the rumble
Of carriage wheels and
Saw black plumed horses,
Stepping solemnly over
Rain-wet cobble stone.

'I have stockings of silk,
And shoes of soft green
Leather...' And I saw then,
Alone at the grave mouth, a
Woman, tall, austere, a
Fine veil darkening her eyes.
And as I watched, she let slip
Into the waiting earth –
One red rose from her hand.
'Combs to buckle my hair

And a ring for every finger.'
In such unbidden images, as
These, seductive and obscure,
I glimpsed a paradox at the
Heart of life – a sorrow

Folded beneath the daily
Round of work and pleasure:
A cross-stitch between death
And love, not personal to
You but threaded into the

Fabric of things. I
Could not know where your
Thoughts travelled while
You sang these songs or what
Their import was exactly
But I recognised the mood
And cadence and sensed
That you mourned something
Abandoned in becoming this
Woman, this wife, who stood

By a window singing –
Some freedom or the dream
Of it – a self owned in an
Earlier existence (at home
With five sisters) a life
Lived out before this one
Was conceived. And hearing
The elegant regret in the
Lines, 'silver buckles are
Fine and silken clothes

Are bonny but I would
Trade them all...' I
Knew that my attendance
At your kitchen table,
Alert and quiet over
Colouring book and crayons –
Was for you, at once,
The emblem of this
Unspoken loss, its seal –
And its consolation.

Making Small Talk.

1.

Where do I live?
you ask.
You tell me –
I say.
In my own house?
You tell me –
Is it beside the sea?
you ask.
You tell me –
Is it called something?
You tell me –
What is it?
You tell me –
If it is, you say
I hope that it's
not 'Seaview'?
Why not? I ask
Well –
it would be such
an obvious name –
wouldn't it –
'Seaview'?
you say.

2.

I phone you every day
and hear your
other-world voice
echoing down
the telephone wires.
Hello Mary Brigid
is that you?

And where is this I am?
you ask.
And where is this you are?
When I tell you
you're astonished,
Are you quite sure?
you say.
I thought it was years
since I was here
or you were there.

3.

Forty one years ago,
when my father died,
my terror
was that you
might follow him,
that I would
lose the two
of you –
you too
my favourite.
Yet here you are
past ninety –
forty one years
after his death
hanging on
for dear life.
And not for any
particular reason,
you say –
it's extraordinary,
I don't know why –
it's not as if
I'm trying!

4.

Do you remember
your father?
you ask
every time
we talk.
Yes, I say
every time.
What do you remember?
you ask.
When I tell you –
listing all the things
I can think of
in chronological order –
from the feel of his suits,
to the smell of his skin,
to the names of the books
that he read to us,
You stare at me
open mouth.
You are incredulous
and dismayed.
How can anyone
you ask –
remember so much
about one person?
Even their father!

5.

You can't tell me
what you've done
today,
or where you are
or who you're with.
You can't tell me

if you've just
had lunch
or are on your way
to bed.
There's no point,
you say, briskly
in asking me –
my mind
has gone to pot
completely!
But you can tell me
who you are –
I insist
And you can
tell me
who I am,
I say.
Yes.
So, you do remember
something?
Yes, you say,
that's true. And
as someone else
said
about beauty
and truth –
That is all
I know –
and all I
need to know!

Frost

And here you are now,
on the threshold –
half a ghost
already.
In the long corridors
of your mind
you pace,
haunting yourself.

Your eyes gaze out
from uncurtained
windows.
Damp has risen
through the bare boards
and seeped into
your voice.

And look –
along the pathway
that led to the sea –
on the grass
and on the hedges,
a first frost has formed.
It glitters on
your hair
and skin.

Snow

You call to me
now,
across a ghost filled
continent.
I see your breath
whitening
the air.
You are calling
goodbye.
You are too far off
for me to hear
distinctly
but I see
that you are
waving –
your hand
raised.

You will stand
alone
on the granite step,
the sea
at your feet,
the door thrown
open behind you –
all the beloved dead
gathered
at your shoulder.

You will stand there
waving,
your hand raised,
waving goodbye –

until you have
gone
from sight
completely.
And even the tracks
in the snow,
that led
to your life,
have vanished.

Testing the Waters

You stand
a little breathless
on the brink,
gripping the rail.
You are brightly
dressed
for the occasion –
a summer frock,
a cardigan over
your shoulders.

In one hand
you carry
an over-night bag,
in the other
the mask
of your face.
You slip it
on and off,
for effect –
now tears,
now laughter.

You teeter
forward
in small steps,
shyly adjusting
your costume.
You skirt
the ice-cream stand
and the lifeguard's
hut, with a genial
drinker's

wave of the hand,
and blithe
disregard
for impediments.

On the narrow
bank, finally,
the deck-chairs
are folded –
the day-trippers
flown.
You pause to study
your wrist watch,
you have the time
exactly, but
have you the day?
There is no one left
now,
to confirm it.

Gathering
purpose,
with an antique
gesture,
you spread
a cotton
handkerchief
and kneel
to lift off
your shoe.
Gingerly,
you reach
the fine
bone china
of your heel,
to test the chill

waters —
with near
veteran poise.

I see you there
still,
on the white sands —
straw hat —
black veil.
Standing —
the last light
behind you —
one foot in —
one foot out
of the river
to death.

Smiling at me —
my ghost mother.

TWO

The Rapture of Senses

These Days of Languor

These days of languor –
loosed of everything
but pleasure
and time.

Enthral to sense,
we put on clothes
only at late evening.
One moment

leading to the next
and back again.
At last,
light fading

on the balcony,
we spread a cloth
and eat –
oysters,

avocado,
new strawberries.
In candle flame, as
you lift your glass

I see love's stain –
wine red
under your
fingernails.

Nocturne

How we sleep these days!
Hours of it.
Like winter creatures

Underground.
Night steeped.
No time for talk,

No time for sex.
Just work
And then sleep.

Hours of it –
From last light
To dawn.

Swimmers
Underwater,
Fathomless among

Reed and coral. Waves
Of unconsciousness
Breaking in dream –

Blue upon blue –
Hours of it,
Doused.

Then –
Once or twice,
Up for air –

Nearer to surface
Or deeper,
All at once,

Night shifts —
Sense,
The satin cool

Of your thigh
Against mine —
Such delight!

Summer

Lake water
at our heels,
the travelling sky
in our ears,
we lay
in summer grasses
long –
and kissed
until the cows
came home.

The Rapture of Senses

Love —
is not only
the love of the body —
the rapture of senses.
It is also

Work,
and forbearance.
Hoping
against hope.
Turning a blind eye,

Holding the tongue.
Speaking out
when it's dangerous.
It is impetuous,
foolish,

Quick witted,
incautious,
letting the heart
rule the head.
It is forgetting

Offense,
forgoing dignity.
Falling out,
reconciling.
It is being alike

And being various,
agreeing
to disagree,
or taking the trouble
to fight.

It is thinking
the same thought
in different places.
Or in the one place,
looking silently

In contrary directions.
It is cooking
for two, at evening
when only one
is hungry.

Or wakeful in the
small hours,
quiet, while
the other sleeps.
It is laughing aloud

For no reason.
Weeping
in secret,
for the others
grief.

Love –
is not only
the love of the body –
the rapture of senses.
But if it were this

And nothing more –
it would be love
enough –
my love,
for one lifetime.

Waking

I like the mornings
When I wake
And know
It's one of those mornings.
A morning when we wake
In the same bed.
I lean over
Your face
And wait
For you to wake
And look at me.
I wait to see
It shine
From your eyes –
The memory
That it's one
Of those mornings –
When I wait
For you to wake.

Angels at Play

We two —
original pair —
own not one
belonging
in common.
Not so much
as a cup
or a chair.

You and I
never say
we —
and mine
seldom blurs
into ours.
Bizarre
for me

Who used to
pool, every
possession
and tool.
Curtains and
cookers
paintings,
and plants,

Dogs and cars
and cats
and debts.
Now, I've
grown nervous
of buying for
two, even
bathroom

Or garden
equipment. And
window-shopping
my legs shake,
pricing
duvet covers
and crockery.
But you too,

Are a spirit
of sky –
recovering
slowly
joy in flight –
recently escaped
from the latest
and last,

Domestic
clipped wings
regime. And so,
together we
keep ourselves
clear of
material bonding –
the frame of

Things, spare,
the furniture
plain.
But once
fired from
this atmosphere –
high
in the element

Of air, we
soar into our
own cool blue
belonging
up there.
At one
in the ether,
sexy –

Mischievous –
unfettered –
like angels
at play –
skin bathing in
the stratosphere.
And who cares
then –

As we fly in the
face of things –
that on earth
we share not one
thing together
unless it's
a book,
a bath –

Or a bed.
What matter
then, as we
cavort, unowned
in spaciousness
we two –
you and I –
original pair.

Strong Tea

I like it when I'm upstairs
and you're downstairs

and you call up
do you want some tea?

I like being downstairs
making tea –

not bothering to call up.
Knowing you'll want some

when you see mine.

Heaven's Breath Held

There are so many
things,
I haven't said
about love
or trying to love.
I've said so much
about the body
and bed –

and even now
when I'm trying –
I could get waylaid
there instead.
There are so many
things
I've never written
about why we want

to love,
or want to try
to find happiness
in affection
that's romantic
and sexual.
And it is not
that I haven't

failed or been
failed by –
over and again,
all the usual
large reasons why.
It isn't that
I haven't
asked myself

what it signifies
in the first
place —
this love word
of ours,
so often used
without intention
that it means

almost nothing
that isn't banal
or a lie.
If I draw up
a list
of the things
we might know it by —
attributes

we call on
to mark it from
mere physical lust
and infatuations.
The high sounding
virtues — out of the
nineteenth century —
such as fidelity,

charity (which
ought to begin
at home but rarely
does) faith
and constancy —
If these grand
abstractions are
the measure

of loving,
then it is all
too plain, that
I've been betrayed
more than once –
by each one of them.
And that I,
in my turn,

have proved
faithless,
time and again
to both letter
and spirit.
So what is it
I mean when I say –
I love?

What is it
I've found there,
in that perilous
country
that isn't to be got
on charted paths,
or in other
affections

more orderly?
One thing stands
clear – numinous
for me,
something too often
forgotten
when
talking of grief
and desertion.

All the let down
and anger,
and wounding,
and blame
that comes with
the heart's
inconsistency.

One thing flames
high –
lambent
above the debris,
and throughout it
for years.
Joy is the thing –
one grace

I could name
that love has
brought round
more or less
regularly.
The one guest
that turns up
in the heart

unannounced,
that cannot be
planned for
predicted
or rationed.
Joy – is
the essence
that gets lost

in translation,
from poetry
to prose,
from passion
to caring.
That can't be found
anywhere
without danger.

Joy that frequents
the conception
of risk and dies
in the fine print
of contract.
If any one of you
knows of anything
that gives more

radiance
or more often,
in kind or degree
than what we call
love —
romantic and sexual
then I wish you
joy of it —

but I haven't.
There are so many
things
I've never written
about love or
attempting to love.
(I've said so much
about the body

and bed and
even now
when I'm trying
I could get waylaid
there instead
by thoughts of
your skin
or your hair.)

I've said so much
yet neglected
to mention
one last aspect
surely
fundamental
to the whole
that I might call

metaphorically
speaking –
the sleeping
partner of love
(silent as often
as not.)
Empathy is the
quality to which

I'm referring
by which I
intend
among many things –
the sensation
of joy
in sharing –
for where it exists –

the practice of
empathy
(as much the gift
of time as feeling)
there is joy
in the knowledge
or expectation —
that when one

confides
another attends
in that particular
manner —
(at once,
in the nerve
of the issue)
possible

only
after the chrism
of spilt blood
and sweat
and tears
of attrition.
This then,
is it —

what I mean
to say, that
the joy of passion —
its labour —
that conjoining
of the senses;
of pleasure
and pain,

of the pulse
and mind –
bestows
the power,
sometimes
to break loose
abruptly as
from chrysalis,

the transient
ghost
of earthly
communion.
And there,
in the hush
of after birth –
as though, one

of God's annointed –
for a moment
or two –
heaven's breath held –
a lover may speak,
and believe that
a kindred soul
listens.

Keeping Vigil

It is not that the world
Is safer –
Wars ravage as usual. Children
Die unnoticed, in our sleep.
Along the same fragrant roads,
Between the olive groves
And that gilded sea –
Where we first embraced –
Women are herded to slaughter.

It is not that the sky
Shelters us,
From loss or betrayal
Or prophecies of storm.
It is not that the days
Are longer, or that the
Stars can pierce
The sulphurous city nights.

It is not that our lives
Are easy –
Our best work thwarted
Our language scarred –
It is not that comforts
Make comfortable,
That love endures,
Or that any of us
Will escape our fate –
These tracks of iron
Laid on sleepers, run
In one direction only.

It is not the moments
Of epiphany – the unlooked
For transfigurations

Of the earthly — such as,
On a frozen field
Where we stopped to kiss —
Emerging from a snow-bound
Wood, a herd of deer —
Suddenly —
Their antlers blown like
Driftwood on a white lake.

It is not that the world
Is better — (beyond the
Perimeter wire, you too,
Hear the cries that fret
The edge of silence.)
It is only that you kept
Vigil, with me, here,
On this station platform,
Waiting for change,
Or for light. That hour
After hour you stared
Into the blizzard mouth —
Watching for a sign of thaw.

It is not that the world
Is safer —
Yet, in darkness, you fall
Asleep at my side, and when
You wake, the day opens with
You; startled, mercurial —
Like a first morning,
Making breakfast or love.
Quick to laughter,
To argument and surprise.
It is not that the world
Is safer. Only this —
That I love your laughter.

Grace

When you turn
your back
to me —
back comes

The first day
to me.
The first
time

I loved you
and saw
that long line
sweep

From shoulder
to flank.
As in
Japanese

Calligraphy —
one brush
stroke,
defining —

A precise
statement
of
grace.

THREE

Time Has Made A Mirror

Time Has Made a Mirror

Sometimes,
I stretch my hands
to the light.
Wanting
to see you again.

Time has made them
a mirror.
It seems
in your absence,
they have grown

To resemble yours –
taken your shape,
your attitudes.
Or is it,
only,

The wide bands
of silver
that I wear now
on the third finger
of each hand

That gives them
this air
of reflecting yours?
Is it time?
Or these pieces

Of silver
that has made them
a mirror –
of your strength?
Your suffering?

Shoulder

I must
in all
those
years –
a thousand
times
or more,

have crossed
a room –
and stood
behind her
to lay
a kiss –
on the flesh
of her
shoulder.

How many times?
Countless –
times without
number –
because
all
these
years
later,

my lips
still –
feel
the
impress –
of her cool,
naked
shoulder.

Once

Once
your name
performed miracles.

I had only
to pronounce it
and you answered

With your presence.
Spoken into a telephone –
Five minutes later

There you were
at the gate.
Called out

As you left me –
you turned back
on the stairs.

Whispered between
sheets
the heat of your body

Enfolded mine.
Once
your name

Performed miracles.
Now
its six letters

Summon only
silence.
Its three syllables

Hang in the air
beautiful,
idle,

altering nothing.
Your name
was a rope

Stretched between us
for years.
Taut or slack –

It bound us –
sound to sight.
A rope stretched

Between us.
I held onto my end.
You let go.

We call it love.

In Your Shoes

When you were gone
I found a pair of shoes

you had left behind
under the bed.

I put them on, wanting
to know how they felt.

The leather was worn
and intimate,

loose across the instep.
I walked to the window

and then to the door.
My heel slipped free

but the toes pinched.
I wanted to see how

it felt in your shoes –
constrained or easy.

I wanted to see
how it felt to be you –

when you wore them and
walked free of me.

Blood

When I weep –

I taste blood
in my mouth.

I reach a hand
to my heart –

It still beats.

Learning by Heart

What am I to do
with my loss of you?
What good can I put it to?
I must do something

Before it kills me. If
I am not to see you again
in this world, still
I can make some use of you.

I can assemble you –
piece by piece,
lay you out –
every aspect and grace

Once loved,
arranged and numbered,
your form and features
observed in motion

And stillness.
I can research memory –
reconstruct your image;
each part played,

The day and time of year
The costumes you wore,
your gestures, every turn
of the head and phrase.

If I am not to see you
again in this world
still I can find some
use for you –

Standing in the wings
for one last curtain call –
like a good understudy –
I can learn you by heart.

Endless Days

I miss
the endless days –
emptying
one
into the other.
Piling up at the window
like rain.
Or snow.

I miss
the hills
flushed
crimson at evening –
and at day break
clouds stalking
the drenched fields.

I miss
the quarrels
and the laughter.
The stillness.
A favourite chair
by the fire.

I miss
the sight of you –
your eyes,
your hands,
your knees.
The sight of you.

I miss
the endless days
emptying
one into another.
Time
piling up at the window
like snow.

And now,
in a foreign street
when rain begins
and someone says –
Let's make for home,
I miss a house
I turn towards still.

About the Author

The award winning short story writer, poet and novelist, Mary Dorcey was born in County Dublin, Ireland. In 1990 she won the Rooney Prize for Literature for her short story collection *A Noise from the Woodshed*.

Her best selling novel *Biography of Desire* (Poolbeg) was published in September of 1997 to critical acclaim and reprinted three months later, and is now about to go into its third reprint.

In 1990 she published a novella, 'Scarlet O'Hara' (1990) contained in the anthology *In and Out of Time* (Onlywomen Press). She has published three volumes of poetry: *Kindling* (Only Women Press, 1982), *Moving into the Space Cleared by Our Mothers* (Salmon Publishing, 1991), and *The River That Carries Me* (Salmon Publishing, 1995).

She has been awarded three Art Council Bursaries for literature, in 1990 and 1995 and 1999. Her work is now taught on Irish Studies and Women's Studies courses in universities internationally. Several theses have been published on her work and numerous critical essays.

Her stories and poems have been anthologized in more than one hundred collections. Her poetry is taught on both the Irish Junior Certificate English course and on the British O Level English curriculum. It has been performed on radio and television (R.T.E. and Channel 4.) It has also been dramatized for stage productions in Ireland, Britain and Australia in *In the Pink* (The Raving Beauties) and *Sunny Side Plucked*.

For over fifteen years she has given talks and readings of her work at major art festivals and at universities and book shops throughout Ireland, Britain and Europe, and the United States.

She has lived in The United States, England, France, Spain and Japan.

She is at present a Research Associate at Trinity College Dublin. She is writer in residence at the Centre for Gender and Women's Studies where she gives seminars in contemporary English literature and leads a creative writing workshop.